W9-BZC-178

Maggie
and the
Monster

Maggie

and the

Monster

Elizabeth Winthrop • Tomie dePaola

G. P. PUTNAM'S SONS

For Maggie Spencer Field, who told me all about her monster. —E. W.

For Maggi and her monster, Carlton. —T. deP.

G. P. PUTNAM'S SONS
A division of Penguin Young Readers Group.
Published by The Penguin Group.

Penguin Group (USA) Inc., 375 Hudson Street, New York, NY 10014, U.S.A. Penguin Group (Canada), 90 Eglinton Avenue East, Suite 700, Toronto, Ontario, Canada M4P 2Y3 (a division of Pearson Penguin Canada Inc.). Penguin Books Ltd, 80 Strand, London WC2R 0RL, England. Penguin Ireland, 25 St. Stephen's Green, Dublin 2, Ireland (a division of Penguin Books Ltd.). Penguin Group (Australia), 250 Camberwell Road, Camberwell, Victoria 3124, Australia (a division of Pearson Australia Group Pty Ltd). Penguin Books India Pvt Ltd, 11 Community Centre, Panchsheel Park, New Delhi - 110 017, India. Penguin Group (NZ), Cnr Airborne and Rosedale Roads, Albany, Auckland 1310, New Zealand (a division of Pearson New Zealand Ltd). Penguin Books (South Africa) (Pty) Ltd, 24 Sturdee Avenue, Rosebank, Johannesburg 2196, South Africa. Penguin Books Ltd, Registered Offices: 80 Strand, London WC2R 0RL, England.

ISBN 978-0-399-24711-8

Every night, a monster came into Maggie's room.

She crashed into the furniture.

She crawled under the table.

She sat down on the chair and grumbled to herself.
Maggie didn't like the monster.
"GET OUT OF MY ROOM!" she shouted.

But the monster didn't pay attention.
She just pushed her big hairy feet
around on the floor and sighed.
Maggie turned over and went to sleep.

"A monster comes into my room at night,"
Maggie told her mother.

"What does it look like?" her mother asked.
"She's got big hairy feet," Maggie said.

"I wonder why she likes your room so much,"
said her mother.
"There's a monster in the upstairs closet too,"
Maggie said. "She sits in the corner behind the brooms."
"Really?" her mother said. "I never noticed."

That night, Maggie hung a sign on her doorknob.
It read:

MAGGIE'S
ROOM
MONSTERS
KEEP OUT!

But the monster paid no attention.
She just banged the door open and marched right in.

"Can't you read?" Maggie asked in a loud voice.
The monster didn't answer.

She snuffled around under the bed
and peeked behind the curtains.

She knocked some books off the shelf.
"WATCH OUT," Maggie shouted.

"You are the clumsiest monster I've ever met."
The monster didn't pay any attention.
She sat down in the same old chair
and grumbled to herself.
Maggie stared at her for a long time.
Then she turned over and went to sleep.

"The monster came back last night,"
Maggie told her mother.
"I think she's looking for something."
"Why don't you ask her?" her mother said.
"That's a good idea," Maggie said.

That night, when the monster walked in,
Maggie sat up in bed.
"Hi, monster," she said.
The monster shuffled up and stared at Maggie.
"Hello."

"What do you want?" Maggie asked.
"I'm looking for my mother,"
the monster said.
"Why didn't you tell me that before?"
Maggie said. "Come with me."

She took the monster by the hand
and led her down the hall.
The monster in the closet
peeked out from behind the brooms.
"This must be your mother," Maggie said.
"She has big hairy feet just like yours."

"Mama!" the monster cried.
"My baby!" said the mother monster.

Maggie left them alone together
and went back to bed.